In *Kinky Hair is Kingly Hair*, Mansa is at it again. This time he's out to set the record straight, proclaiming that whether you refer to it as "kinky" or "nappy," this type of textured hair is synonymous with royalty.

Kinky Hair is Kingly Hair

by Dynast Amir

illustrated by Yashar Clemons

Foreword

One of the greatest things in life are the differences and similarities we share. Many things in life make us unique, interesting, and different. However, there are also common traits and characteristics that help us identify with others that share our history, heritage, and culture.

Our differences with one another should be used as learning opportunities to discover stories about our ancestors, and teach us about the traits that identify us as a people. They should never be used to separate us from others but should always bring us closer to others.

Our history is a royal pedigree, as we are descendants of kings and queens from a tropical land and a vast continent rich in gold, minerals, & natural resources. Our hair is one of our resources given to us by our ancestors that represents God's fingerprint of creation.

Many crowns have rested atop a head of lambs wool. From Hallie Sellasie, to Shaka Zulu, Jesus Christ, & also You! That's right, your hair is a trait of African Royalty. We all know what they did with their crowns, what will you do with yours?

-Theida Salazar

"Take the kinks out of your mind,
not your hair."

Marcus Garvey

"Kinky Hair is Kingly Hair,"as
you can see.
Many kings had kinky hair just
like me.

Hannibal of Carthage
brought Rome to its knees.

Imhotep built some of the
first colleges and universities.

Shaka Zulu conquered his
enemies with ease.

Malcolm X pledged, "By any means necessary!"

Egyptians were the first to harness electricity!

St. Maurice led the Catholic
Church to victory.

Kwame Nkrumah preached a doctrine of Pan African unity.

Thomas Sankara sacrificed so his people can have their necessities.

Toussaint L'Overture fought for the independence of Haiti.

Mansa Musa paved streets of gold from Mecca to Mali.

Nelson Mandela marched to
end apartheid.

Abubakari, before Columbus, discovered a new land on the other side of the great sea.

So fade it, edge it, lock it down.

You are royalty, so protect
your crown!

Wherever you go, proclaim it loud.

"Kinky Hair is Kingly Hair!"

How beautiful the sound.

The End

Kinky Hair is Kingly Hair

Author's Notes

I wrote this book to commemorate the ancestors whom were specifically chosen by God to give birth to civilization as we know it, in a place now called Africa. This work serves as a bridge, connecting the youth of today with our ancestors. The connection lies much deeper than just the words and illustrations found throughout this work. It can be found on the head of every black person that has set foot on this planet. Rather you prefer nappy hair, because nappy hair is happy hair. Some may call it natural, for natural hair is one with nature. I call it kinky, because it harmonizes with kingly. Often times, the uniqueness of black hair is misunderstood, belittled and mocked. In our unique hair, lies our strength. Kinky hair is an important physical trait that connects every black man and woman to the original people whom inhabited this earth first. No one else on this planet has kinky hair.

- The pyramids were built by those who had kinky hair.
- The richest man to have ever lived had kinky hair.
- The first people to have performed surgeries and discover vaccines had kinky hair.
- The first universities were built by kinky haired individuals.
- The first major metropolises were built by those with kinky hair.
- The first kings that ruled earth had kinky hair.

So this message is intended for every young black boy and black girl. "Kinky Hair is Kingly Hair!", how beautiful the sound.

Allow me to first give thanks to the ancestors, my mom and dad. A special thanks to Natalia, Yashar, Theida and Atim for assisting in making this book a reality.

Dynast Amir was born in Sacramento, CA. He found his passion for writing through journaling everyday. Dynast has been consistently traveling to Africa since 2011, and plans on relocating to Nigeria and Sierra Leone soon. His ambition in life is to purchase lands for afflicted souls and to possess more gold than Mansa Musa. Dynast currently serves as the Omo Oba "Prince" of Ororuwo, Nigeria and invites everyone to come and visit the Kingdom of Ororuwo one day.

Kinky Hair is Kingly Hair

Yashar Clemons is a native of Los Angeles, CA. Just recently graduating from Chico State University in Chico, California, he is in the process of debuting his own comic book series. Yashar's ambition is to be a professional animator and to uplift souls through art. In accomplishing this, he believes that he will experience true happiness. "I want to make a living doing what I love to do best."

Kinky Hair is Kingly Hair

Manufactured in the United States of America

ISBN: 978-1-7346383-2-5

Publisher/Author contact: info@noirisme.com

For information regarding discounts or bulk purchases, please visit our website or email info@noirisme.com

Kinky Hair is Kingly Hair

Made in the USA
San Bernardino, CA
25 May 2020